Topic: Family   **Subtopic:** Divorce

Notes to Parents and Teachers:

As a child becomes more familiar reading books, it is important for him/her to rely on and use reading strategies more independently to help figure out words they do not know.

REMEMBER: PRAISE IS A GREAT MOTIVATOR!

Here are some praise points for beginning readers:

- I saw you get your mouth ready to say the first letter of that word.
- I like the way you used the picture to help you figure out that word.
- I noticed that you saw some sight words you knew how to read!

Book Ends for the Reader!

Here are some reminders before reading the text:

- Point to each word you read to make it match what you say.
- Use the picture for help.
- Look at and say the first letter sound of the word.
- Look for sight words that you know how to read in the story.
- Think about the story to see what word might make sense.

Words to Know Before You Read

change

divorce

father

flowers

lives

mother

parents

together

Forever Rhen
A Story About Divorce

By Sandra Athans

Illustrated by
John Joseph

Rourke
Educational Media
rourkeeducationalmedia.com

Rhen lived in a home by a hill.

She liked to play on the hill with her parents.

"Up we go!" said her mother.

"Down we go!" said her father.

Rhen liked the flowers on the hill.

She gave some to her mother.
She gave some to her father.

One day Rhen was told of a change.

Her parents would not be together like before. They were getting a divorce.

"We will share our Rhen,"
said her mother.

"Yes, take turns with our Rhen," said her father.

Now Rhen lives with her mother.

"Up we go!" says her mother.

Rhen lives with her father, too.

"Down we go!" says her father.

Rhen gives flowers to her mother.

Rhen gives flowers to her father.

A lot has changed, but Rhen is the same.

She is Rhen forever and she is loved!

Book Ends for the Reader

I know...

1. What did Rhen give to her parents?

2. What changed in Rhen's life?

3. What did not change in Rhen's life?

I think...

1. Do you know someone whose parents are divorced?

2. What are some things a kid might worry about if their parents are not together?

3. How can parents help kids feel better if they decide to divorce?

Book Ends for the Reader

What happened in this book?

Look at each picture and talk about what happened in the story.

About the Author

Sandra Athans is a writer and a teacher. She has a special trick to cheer up her students whenever they're feeling a little uneasy. What's her trick? She sings a silly song! It works every time! Think of a silly song you know, and try for yourself.

About the Illustrator

John Joseph's passion for art appeared at an early age, while living in Orlando, Florida. As a young boy, he was inspired by the many trips to visit the animation studios just down the road at the happiest place on Earth.

Library of Congress PCN Data

Forever Rhen (A Story About Divorce) / Sandra Athans
(Changes and Challenges In My Life)
ISBN 978-1-64156-494-6 (hard cover)(alk. paper)
ISBN 978-1-64156-620-9 (soft cover)
ISBN 978-1-64156-731-2 (e-Book)
Library of Congress Control Number: 2018930711

Rourke Educational Media
Printed in the United States of America,
North Mankato, Minnesota

Edited by: Keli Sipperley
Layout by: Rhea Magaro-Wallace
Cover and interior Illustrations by: John Joseph